The Case
of the
Dirty Bird

YEARLING BOOKS/YOUNG YEARLINGS/YEARLING CLASSICS are designed especially to entertain and enlighten young people. Patricia Reilly Giff, consultant to this series, received her bachelor's degree from Marymount College and a master's degree in history from St. John's University. She holds a Professional Diploma in Reading and a Doctorate of Humane Letters from Hofstra University. She was a teacher and reading consultant for many years, and is the author of numerous books for young readers.

For a complete listing of all Yearling titles,
write to Dell Readers Service,
P.O. Box 1045, South Holland, IL 60473.

Gary Paulsen

The Case of the Dirty Bird

A YEARLING BOOK

Published by
Dell Publishing
a division of
Bantam Doubleday Dell Publishing Group, Inc.
666 Fifth Avenue
New York, New York 10103

ISBN: 0-440-40598-X

Printed in the United States of America

July 1992

10 9 8 7 6 5 4 3 2 1

OPM

The Case
of the
Dirty Bird

Chapter · 1

Duncan—Dunc—Culpepper sat on the corner of the window and looked at the parrot in the cage hanging from the ceiling on a rusty chain.

"It smells like my uncle Alfred's feet when he takes his shoes off to pick his toes," Amos Binder said. He was Dunc's best friend, had been forever, and was staying well back from the parrot. "I wish he didn't do that."

"What?" Dunc thought he was talking about the parrot. Which wasn't doing anything. He wondered if it was dead. No. There, the eye moved. It was alive. Just.

1

"Pick his feet. He comes over for dinner whenever he gets hungry, and after he eats he sits with my father in the living room and watches football and takes his shoes off and picks his feet through the socks. You know. I wish he didn't do that. It makes dinner hard to hold down."

"Tell him next time that his feet smell like a parrot."

"Right. I tell him anything, and he'll knuckle my forehead like he did last time he thought I smarted off. I couldn't focus my right eye for half a day." Amos looked at the rest of the pet store. "Why are we here, anyway? Melissa Hansen is due to walk past my place on her way home from her dance lessons. I was thinking that if I stood just right, she would notice me. I'm pretty sure she called me last week—"

"We're here because of the contest."

"—at least I think it was her. The phone rang and I ran for it, but I stepped on the cat, which shouldn't have been sleeping in the doorway, and that made me trip over the coffee table and jam my head under the end table with my mouth around the elec-

2

trical outlet. I think I would have made it if I hadn't gotten that shock. I'm pretty sure it was her, even though I only heard a click. It sounded like her click. What contest?"

Dunc was used to Amos talking about his problems getting to the phone. Amos could not get across a room without wrecking it if he thought Melissa Hansen was part of it.

"I told you about it," Dunc said. "I'm entering an essay contest in that wildlife magazine. *National Wildlife.* It's for people under eighteen, and I figure I've got a chance."

"And you're going to write about parrots?"

Dunc nodded.

"Oh, man, why didn't you pick a bird that doesn't stink? What about eagles or hawks or buzzards? I mean, parrots aren't even wild."

"Yes, they are. There are tons of them living in the wild in the jungles. I just can't get to them. So here we are."

He turned back to the parrot. It was green and scruffy, seemed to be missing about half its feathers, and really *did* smell bad.

3

"Can I help you boys?" The owner of the pet store, a tall man who had glasses with a chain around the back of his neck and a pocket full of pens in a plastic case, came over to them.

"I just wondered," Dunc said, "how old this parrot is."

"The provenance does not go back to his birth," the man said. His voice was high and birdlike. Like his nose, Duncan thought. "But we do know he is at least one hundred and four years old. He might be as much as one hundred and fifty."

Amos stared at the parrot. "A hundred and fifty years old?"

"Yes. He's very old—parrots are thought to live a very long time—up to two hundred years. This parrot has belonged to at least ten people and outlived them all."

"Does he talk?" Dunc hadn't heard the parrot make a sound.

"Oh, my, yes. In four languages. Sometimes he mixes them up, and he can swear in all four as well. Some words I'm not sure you should hear."

"It can't be worse than my uncle Alfred," Amos said. "He picks his feet."

"How singular." The pet-store owner looked down his nose at Amos. "In public?"

"No. Just in our living room. I wish he'd stop."

"I can imagine."

"How do you get him to talk?" Duncan asked.

"You must talk to him—and he must be in the mood."

"Polly want a cracker?" Amos asked the bird. The parrot looked at him, belched, and went to the bathroom all over the bottom of the cage.

"Oh, man, that's gross." Amos turned away. "What do you feed him?"

"Special seeds and shells and a wheat paste that he favors. Now, don't you two bother him. He's a very valuable bird, and we don't want to upset him."

"How much is he worth?" Dunc asked.

"He's for sale for eleven thousand dollars."

"Eleven thousand dollars?" Amos turned back. "For something that smells that bad?

I'll bet you could buy my uncle Alfred for that—and he knows more words than the parrot. Well, maybe."

The pet-store owner had turned away, and Amos pulled at Dunc's sleeve. "Come on."

"Just a minute." Dunc held back. "I want to hear him talk."

"He's not going to talk."

The parrot belched again—opened its beak wide—almost a yawn and said a word that Dunc had heard in the bus depot when two old winos were arguing over a bottle in a paper sack.

"See?" Dunc said. "He talks."

"Right—just like Uncle Alfred." Amos pulled on Dunc. "Let's leave."

"All right, but we have to come back tomorrow."

"Why?"

"I don't know—there's just something about the bird." Dunc studied the parrot. "Something weird."

"Oh, man, don't do this—the last time you looked like that I had to dress up like a puppet and hide in a toy store until some-body tried to steal me."

"What's the matter?" Dunc followed him toward the door. "Didn't you like it?"

"Treasure."

"What?" Duncan tapped Amos on the arm. "What did you say?"

"I didn't say anything."

"You said 'treasure.' "

"Not me."

"Well, somebody did—wait a minute." Dunc turned back into the store and stopped by the parrot's cage again.

"Oh, come on," Amos said. "We're going to be late, and I won't get the chance for Melissa to notice me."

"He said it." Dunc studied the parrot. "I heard him say 'treasure.' "

"You're nuts—I'm going whether you come or not." Amos turned, and as he turned his crazy bone hit the edge of a counter full of pet supplies. He said a word that Dunc had seen written on the side of a rail car.

"Treasure map."

"There!" Dunc said. "He said it again. I

heard him. When you swore, he said 'trea-sure map.' "

Amos was doubled over holding his elbow. "So what?"

But Dunc wasn't listening to him. He was watching the parrot intently.

And he definitely had that look.

Chapter·2

"It's like this," Dunc said.

"Don't say that."

"Don't say what?"

"Don't say, 'It's like this.' " Amos was sitting on their front porch. It was a warm summer afternoon and they were wearing shorts, and he was wondering if he should pick the scab off his knee. He'd gotten it two weeks before trying to get to the phone. He'd been in the bathroom and the phone rang, and he was sure it was Melissa and went for it and would have made it except that his mother had the oven door open and he took a shortcut through the kitchen. He

9

stepped in a cake, broke the oven door off, and buried his head in the cat box in the corner of the kitchen and scraped his knees on the oven door going down. "It's never like 'this' when you say 'it's like this.' It's always like something else."

"About the business with the parrot. I've been thinking."

"You mean the one at the pet store, or Mrs. Burdgett's parakeets?"

"The one at the store. I don't want to think about Mrs. Burdgett's parakeets."

"Right. I don't blame you." Amos nodded. Dunc had found that a neighborhood woman had a dozen or so parakeets, and he thought she could help with his essay so they'd gone to visit. The problem was, she let all the parakeets out of their cages to show how smart they were and the front door had been slightly open. A loose cat had come to the door, seen the crack, and sneaked in. "How do you figure a cat could miss all those parakeets?"

"It was the broom," Dunc said. "Mrs. Burdgett's broom. She was wild with it."

She'd broken most of the lamps, some

knickknacks, a porcelain figure, and a front window, and the two boys had followed the cat out and hadn't been back.

"I've been doing a little research," Dunc said.

"That's how all this started, remember?"

"No, now listen. Parrots are always associated with who?"

"Fertilizer companies?"

"Come on, be serious. Who do you always think of when you think of parrots?"

Amos frowned, thinking. "Well, I guess sailors."

"Yeah—but what *kind* of sailor?"

"One that stinks?"

"Amos . . ."

"All right, I don't know."

"A pirate. You always see parrots on pirates' shoulders, don't you? I mean in pictures and things?"

Amos thought about it, nodded. "All right, sometimes. But you also see them in beer commercials."

"No—not this time. Now listen. Here's this old, old parrot. Maybe a hundred and fifty years old. He's so old—"

"He stinks."

"Amos. Quit that. He's so old he could have belonged to a pirate. We live on a river not too far from an ocean. So what if he belonged to a pirate and the pirate lived a long time ago and maybe he knows something?"

"Like where a buried treasure is, because he said 'treasure map.' Is that what you're saying?"

"Well—it could be."

Amos shook his head. "Remember now, remember what happened the time you bought a metal detector and we were going to find that treasure left by the Spanish conquistadors?"

"So it didn't work out." Dunc shrugged. "I can't always be right."

"Always? *Always* be right? We must have found close to a million old beer cans and bottle caps and nails. I don't remember a single bit of gold from the Spanish conquistadors."

"Well, that was a magazine article. They're not always too dependable."

"And this parrot is?"

"I think so. I mean I think it's worth a shot. He said 'treasure map,' and he seems to respond to certain code words."

"Those 'code words' could get us arrested, or at least get me restricted until I'm about forty. The last time I said the one that I used when I hit my elbow and my dad heard me, I was spitting Ivory for a month."

"I thought he was more progressive than that."

"Right. He's fine on letting me do things alone, but if I swear—well, I'd rather not think about it."

"So I'll do the swearing. You'll see, it'll be different this time."

"Well . . ."

"Come on, let's go back to the pet store and see the parrot again. Maybe the owner has a list of the people who have owned the parrot. That might help. I mean, if it *was* a treasure and we missed it, you'd never forgive yourself."

"Well . . ."

"Then, too, there's Melissa."

"What about her?"

"Well, if you're a millionaire or maybe even more, she might take notice of you."

Amos rubbed the back of his neck. "Yeah. I could get a car, a red sports car, and learn to drive or have somebody drive me until I was old enough for a license. It could work."

And Dunc knew he had him.

Chapter·3

Dunc stared at the parrot.

The parrot stared at Dunc. If anything, it looked worse than it had the time before. It seemed to have lost more feathers and looked to Amos like a large, plucked, *ugly* chicken.

The bottom of the cage was half an inch deep in what the parrot dumped.

And it smelled worse than before.

Dunc tried another word, one he'd seen written on the back of a biker's T-shirt. He whispered it cautiously, looking around the store first to make certain nobody was within hearing range.

The parrot ignored him, looked away, looked back, belched, reached up with one claw, and delicately scratched a runny sore on his neck.

"He's not answering you," Amos said.

"Thanks. I figured that out."

"That's the fourth word you've used. I didn't know you knew that one. What does it mean?"

"I haven't the slightest idea. It was on the back of a biker's jacket, and I didn't think I should stop him and ask."

"Can we go now? I'm worried somebody will see us and think we're crazy—even crazier than we are."

"Maybe . . ."

"What?"

"Maybe it's you. Maybe you have to be the one who says things to him. It's not just the words—he's coded to you. Sometimes they respond to voices, patterns. I read that in research. Maybe you sound like one of his owners—maybe even the pirate."

"No."

"Amos—we've got to try this. It was your

16

voice that made him talk. Just try it once,
and if it doesn't work, we'll go. I promise."

"Just once? And you promise?"

"Absolutely."

"All right." Amos said a word he had
heard his uncle Alfred say when his mother
ran over his foot with the car while backing
out of the garage. Amos did not say it as
loud as Uncle Alfred had said it—Uncle Alfred practically removed paint from sur-
rounding buildings when he yelled it. In-
stead, Amos held his nose, leaned toward
the parrot, and whispered it.

The effect was immediate. The parrot
belched again—about two points on the
Richter scale—and looked directly at Amos
and said:

"Treasure map."

"See? It's you—you're the one!" Dunc almost jumped up and down. "Try another
one."

Amos hesitated. "You said one. . . ."

"Oh, come on, you have to do it now."

Amos knew he was right. He turned his
face away, took another deep breath, held
it, leaned forward, and said one that was in

a movie about two truckers, a herd of wild pigs, and a monster that lived in Cleveland and ate tourists.

Again the effect was instant. The parrot burped, looked at Amos with something close to fondness, and said:

"Boxes of riches, boxes of riches."

Dunc dug frantically in his pockets for paper and a pen. The store owner was out for the afternoon and the woman taking his place was busy with customers, but she took the time to give Dunc a piece of scrap paper and a ball-point.

"Treasure map," the parrot was saying again as Dunc came back, "boxes of riches, boxes of riches, a nineteen sixty-two Chevrolet Impala is only seventeen hundred dollars and is styled just right for you."

"What?" Dunc was writing as fast as he could. "What was that?"

Amos looked at him. "It sounded like a television commercial for a nineteen sixty-two Chevrolet Impala. Weren't they the ones with the big fins?"

"A commercial? What did you say to him?"

18

"Don't come at me like that—it wasn't my fault. I just used the word that's written in Pete Fulner's locker."

"Well, don't use it again."

But it was too late. The parrot only stopped for a moment, burped, then started again.

"Sarah is a lot prettier than Judy, but she wants to get married. General Electric refrigerators are the only ones that self-defrost and save you all that ugly chipping and steaming eight paces in from the tunnel mouth but this is why *I* chose to feed my family Chef Boyardee spaghetti and meatballs."

"There," Dunc said. "What was that?"

"More commercials, I think—refrigerators and canned food and something about girls."

"No, that other thing. Something about eight paces in from the tunnel mouth." Dunc had been writing furiously, trying to get everything the parrot said as soon as he said it, and he'd missed it.

He shook his head. "This is no good.

19

We're going to have to get a cassette recorder and come back."

"Dunc . . ."

"No, really. We're going to miss something if we don't. Let's run home and get my Walkman."

He was out the door before Amos could tell him that the parrot was starting to speak again. Amos followed him, leaving the parrot who was busily explaining the virtues of something called Brylcreem and about how a little dab would do him.

Chapter · 4

The parrot looked at Amos.

Amos looked at the parrot.

Dunc watched the parrot watching Amos. "Go for it."

They had had to wait another day. When they returned to the store, the owner was there again and Dunc decided that he wouldn't like the boys standing in front of the parrot cage whispering and holding up a tape recorder.

"Hit him with a good one."

Amos shook his head. "You're wacko, do you know that?"

"Do it!"

Amos tried one he'd seen written on a girl's tennis shoe at school.

"Willywack?" Dunc said. "What's that?"

"It's a word."

"But it's not the right kind of word."

"Probably the greatest benefit of owning a new nineteen fifty-eight Buick is the status it lends your life," the parrot said. "You can put margarine on it and it tastes just like bread two paces left and one down I think Sharon might go out with me—"

Dunc scrambled to get the recorder going and held it up.

"—diamonds are forever and say what you really want to say if you want really clean, white teeth use Ipana go for the gold smoke Old Gold cigarettes flash, flash, the Japanese have attacked Pearl Harbor follow the line, follow the line twice as much for a nickel too you know Pepsi is the drink for you—"

"Isn't he ever going to shut up?" Amos said.

"Shh. Let him talk." Dunc had an intent

look on his face as he watched the parrot, listening to each word.

"—fresh eggs are eleven cents a dozen and you can clean your drains without a brush use Saniflush—"

For two hours.

Dunc held the recorder up until the cassette ran out, turned the tape over, ran that side until it was gone, and the parrot was still rattling on. Finally, after two and a half hours, when Dunc was on his second tape and Amos was wandering around the store and so bored he had started to watch gerbils, which he hated, and had memorized everything he saw, even the name of a dog wormer medicine, finally, the parrot stopped.

Dunc turned the recorder off. "He's done."

Amos came back over to the cage, smiled maliciously at Dunc, and said a word he'd seen spray-painted on the ceiling of the school bus when they were on a field trip.

"Tickets are on sale now for the Frank

Sinatra concert which is impossible to tell from the real thing I'd walk a mile for a Camel—"

Dunc raised his arm again—it was like lead—and hit the record switch, and Amos wandered off to the video game in the other end of the mall to watch Hank Evvert get creamed by the gorgons on Gorgon Mania.

He'd been there an hour when Dunc walked in. His arm hung limply at his side, the Walkman dangling by the cord.

"He's done," Dunc said.

"I could come and do another word," Amos said.

"No, I mean really done. He started to repeat the original Chevrolet Impala ad. But there's information there, I know it. Now we just have to go home and translate it, get the good stuff out of the commercials."

"Oh, good," Amos said. "We can listen to him again."

But Dunc was already gone, out the door and headed for the exit from the mall.

Amos waited a moment, shook his head, and followed.

It wasn't, he thought, like he had any choice. What if there really *was* pirate treasure?

Chapter·5

"All right, I think we've got something."

Dunc waved a piece of paper and turned away from the desk in his room. He was still wearing the headset for the Walkman, and he took it off.

Amos was sound asleep in the corner of Dunc's bed. He'd been asleep since midnight when he decided the worst thing in the world was probably a parrot.

He opened his eyes, one at a time, thankful that the dream was gone. He'd dreamt he was in a large cage and an enormous parrot had been coming toward him. "What time is it?"

27

Dunc looked at his watch. "Just after eight o'clock. We barely have time for breakfast."

"Before what?"

"We have to go back to the pet store. I have to listen to him one more time to see if I missed anything. You know, I think he's kind of like living history—that bird knows things about what happened."

Amos closed his eyes. "I slept with my shoes on. My feet are like prunes. I'm going back to sleep. You can't go to a pet store with feet like prunes."

But Dunc was up and out of the room before Amos had finished.

He lay with his eyes closed, but it was no use. Sleep didn't come back, and he knew he would have to go. He stood up and walked on his prunelike feet out the door and downstairs.

Dunc was in the kitchen. He had shredded wheat in a bowl and was pouring hot water on it. Then he drained the hot water off, added milk and sugar, and sat down to eat.

Amos shuddered. "Don't you have any Fruit Slams?"

"In the cabinet."

Amos nodded and took them down. Cereal shaped like fruit. They were for kids, but he'd always had them and still liked them.

He sat to eat.

"You look awful," Dunc said, looking up with his mouth full.

"Thank you. I was worried that I might look too good—you know, make you look bad."

"I was just trying to help. You might want to throw some water on your hair before we go. It's all over to one side. You look like Carey Sander's springer spaniel when it gets wet."

"If you don't be quiet, I'm going to kill you."

"Just trying to help."

"Well, stop."

"We have to go to the pet store," Dunc said. "One more time."

"You said that. Something about having to listen to that stupid bird again."

"I have a list of clues now, but I'm not sure it's complete." Dunc finished his cereal. "And besides, they don't mean anything to me."

Amos paused, his mouth full of Fruit Slams. "Clues—aren't clues supposed to mean something?"

"Well. I think they will, but right now they don't. I'm sure it will come to me."

He put his bowl in the sink and headed for the door. "We'll take bikes."

"I don't have my bike here, remember?"

"No problem—you can take my sister's. She's visiting my aunt for two days."

He was gone, and Amos hurried to catch up. "But your sister has one of those little bikes."

"So what? It's got two wheels and a set of handlebars, doesn't it?"

"It's got training wheels."

"Well then, you won't fall. Come on."

"All I can say is, there'd better be a lot of gold in this."

Dunc was already down the street, pedaling slowly, and Amos took Dunc's sister's bike out of the garage. It was purple and had streamers stuck in the end of each handlebar and a little bell that rang with a thumb button.

He paused for a moment, thought of walking to the mall, then shrugged. It was so early, he wouldn't see anybody anyway. Anybody he knew would still be in bed. He jumped on the bike and started to pedal. His knees seemed to come up alongside his ears, and the bike wobbled a bit.

At the corner he turned to follow Dunc, heard a small giggle, and looked up to see Melissa riding by with a girl named Kathryn Welben.

It was there and gone, over so fast that she had vanished around the corner before he could do more than smile stupidly as she went by. He drifted to a stop.

I should have said I was testing it for Dunc's sister, he thought, wishing he could die. No, I should have said I was on a mission in disguise for the CIA and the bike was part of my cover. No, I should have said the bike was part of some alien's body and I was trapped on it by a force field. No, I should have said Dunc forced me to ride it. . . .

"Are you coming or not?" Dunc had come back and was sitting facing him, one foot on the ground, on a normal bike looking normal.

"I just saw Melissa," Amos said. "She met me and I was riding this—this thing."

"So?"

"So she'll never call now."

"Sure she will." Dunc turned to go again.

"She will?"

"Of course—haven't you ever heard of curiosity? She's going to wonder why you were out in the morning riding a kiddie bike around."

He turned and was gone, and Amos started after him and smiled and thought, heck, maybe he's right.

Maybe I should get a Smurf scooter.

Chapter · 6

"Here's the list of clues."

Amos and Dunc were back in Dunc's room. He'd fired up his computer and typed the clues onto the screen in capital letters.

    TREASURE MAP
    EIGHT PACES FROM TUNNEL MOUTH
    FOUR PACES TO LEFT
    TWO HANDLES DOWN
    LOOK FOR THE UNION LABEL

"Look for the union label?" Amos studied it. "I know that—how do I know that?"

"I thought it might have something to do

with the Civil War," Dunc said. "He kind of sang it—'Look for the union label.' Like that. Like a song."

"Oh. Now I remember. That's a commercial to buy union products. You know, to look for the label when you buy."

Dunc erased it from the screen. "All right. Now let's look."

TREASURE MAP
EIGHT PACES FROM TUNNEL MOUTH
FOUR PACES TO LEFT
TWO HANDLES DOWN
SEE THE EYE OF THE MOON

"That's it?" Amos asked. "For all those hours?"

Dunc nodded. "Not much, is it? But we have the list of owners too—or at least the ones the store owner knew about."

The owner of the pet store had been there when they went back and proved to be nicer than they thought he would be. He let them listen to the parrot again—Amos waited until he was out of hearing before he used the code words—and had given them a copy of the list of owners.

"It goes back a long way. There's one woman who had the parrot for forty-five years." Dunc read from the list.

"Harley Crane had it from 1865 to 1890. That's twenty-five years."

Amos was reading over his shoulder. "The problem is that it doesn't say if any of them were pirates."

"Well, it wouldn't, would it?" Dunc snorted. "You think they'd admit it? They used to hang those guys from the yardarm or something. Who'd want to admit he was a pirate and get hung from a yardarm? You have to detect a little." He ran his finger down the list. "See? Here's one in 1848—his name is George Bonney. That sounds sort of piraty, doesn't it?"

Amos shrugged. "I would have thought Pegleg Pete or One-eyed Ned. Something like that."

"Look at this—Bonney lived down by the waterfront on the river. It says he owned a tavern. I mean, that looks promising, doesn't it?"

"What else does it say about him?"

Dunc shook his head. "Nothing. Just the date and that he was a tavern owner along the river. He owned a place called The Devil's Hammer. Come on now, that's perfect, isn't it?" Dunc stood up, closed one eye. "Arrgh, me hearties, let's go down to The Devil's Hammer for a cup of grog."

Amos shook his head. "I think you're stretching it. All you have is a disgusting bird that goes to the bathroom all the time and likes to hear people say things written on the sides of buses and some guy who owned a bar, and now you're imagining pirates and gold and buried treasure."

"Well, I know it's not scientific, but we've got to follow our hunches. This is a hunch."

"Remember the time we followed your hunch and talked the police into arresting a tractor salesman from South Dakota?"

"That was different. He matched the description of one of those check forgers in the post office pictures perfectly."

"No, he didn't. He had both ears and the guy in the picture had half an ear gone, and it was wrong to tell the police you'd seen him breaking into a car."

"Well?"

"Well nothing."

"What if I'd been right? He was only in jail overnight, and I did apologize, didn't I? Besides, this is different. All we have to do is find a tunnel along the river, and we're halfway home."

"Oh—is that all? How do you figure to do that?"

"Simple. We head down to the waterfront and start looking for something that seems to be a tunnel."

He was out the door and gone—as usual —before Amos could point out that the waterfront along the river was one of those places you didn't go.

Amos started to follow and stopped at the door. "Don't they have rats down there as big as rhinos?" he called.

But Dunc was already out of hearing.

Chapter·7

"How hard can it be to find a tunnel?" Amos said, mimicking Dunc's voice. "It's just a big hole, right?"

They had been down by the river for an hour, and Amos was ready to leave. "I saw a rat, over there, by that guy sleeping with his head under a trash bin. At least, I think he was sleeping. Maybe he was dead."

"He wasn't dead," Dunc said. "They pick them up if they die."

"Oh, good. Now I don't have to worry."

"And it wasn't a rat. It was a cat."

"It had a long hairless tail."

"It was a cat with a long hairless tail."

"And a pointed nose."

"And a pointed nose."

"I still think it was a rat."

They were on their bikes—Amos now had his own—and they rode slowly. The river was a gray muck on their left along a scabby dock, and to their right was a row of old buildings nearly half a mile long. Many of them were abandoned, with windows broken out or boarded over with plywood.

"Lots of words painted on the buildings," Amos noted professionally. "If we have to talk to the parrot again."

Dunc rode silently, looking at the buildings.

"What are we looking for?" Amos asked.

"I don't know. I'm kind of hoping it will show itself to me."

But it didn't. They rode the full length of the waterfront until the road trailed off into thick brush and swamp. Dunc turned around and looked back. "It's there. Something is there. I can just feel it."

He started back and Amos followed, looking at the buildings carefully as Dunc did, with absolutely no idea of what to look for.

A tunnel.

A treasure.

Something with paces.

They rode the full length again until they were starting up the street that left the waterfront and went back into the city. It was by now late afternoon, and Dunc turned his bike again.

"I don't think we should go back again," Amos said. "Some of those people are starting to notice us. I think even the guy with his head under the trash bin looked at me on that second run."

"I just know we're missing something. It's there—we've got to go back."

"Before we do this, I want you to think about it. You're risking our lives over something a dirty bird told you."

Dunc thought for a moment. "All right— I thought about it. Let's go."

They went down the row one more time, pausing in front of each old building, riding fast past a tavern called The Blue Marble, and when they got to the dead end and saw nothing, even Dunc admitted defeat.

"All right. You win. Let's go home and forget it."

And on the way back Amos found it.

They weren't even riding slow. In fact, Amos was pedaling about as fast as he'd ever pedaled because just as they passed The Blue Marble, a man came through the window end over end. He hit the ground and lay still.

Just after The Blue Marble, Amos saw it.

He didn't say anything and kept riding, following Dunc, who had gone to a lower gear and increased his cadence, and they were at the end of the waterfront street where it curved up into the city when Amos couldn't stand it any longer.

"All right. Let's stop."

Dunc slowed, squeezed the brakes, stopped. "What's the matter?"

Amos looked at the sky. "I know I'm going to hate myself for this—I saw something."

"What?"

"I'm not sure. But on a board on a building two doors down from The Blue Marble, just after they threw that guy through the window—I thought I saw something drawn there, or painted. It was old and really faint."

"What was it?"

"I think it was the outline of a hammer painted red. Of course, it probably doesn't mean anything."

But Dunc had turned his bike and was pedaling back down the waterfront street.

"A *thank you* would have been nice," Amos said, turning around. His bike tire seemed to catch on something, and he pushed forward to get over it and heard a sudden hissing. He looked down to see the tire going flat on a broken whiskey bottle.

"Oh, great—Dunc, wait up. I've got a flat," he yelled, but Dunc didn't hear him.

Amos started pushing his bike, looking down between each building for a rat as big as a rhino to come out and run over him.

Chapter · 8

Amos hadn't gone very far when he heard somebody yelling and looked to see Dunc coming back up the street. Two men were chasing him, but they turned away when they saw they couldn't catch up to him.

"What's their problem?" Amos asked when Dunc stopped next to him.

"Oh—they wanted to borrow my bike. Forever." He caught his breath. "I saw it—it's definitely a hammer. I could see the outline. I don't see how I missed it the first few times. I think I could see some lettering, too, but it might have been my imagination. We'll have to come back later—"

"Don't say it," Amos said.

"—after dark."

"That's what I meant. Don't say that. I mean, if we come back here after dark, nobody will ever hear from us again. This is the *waterfront*, Dunc—not your yard. There are people down here who will sell us for medical experiments."

"Well," Dunc said, "you can't expect us to come here in the daylight again, can you? I mean, those guys were throwing bottles at me."

Amos started pushing his bike home, and Dunc pushed his alongside.

"That's hard logic to beat," Amos said. "How about if we don't come down here at all?"

"You don't mean that."

"I don't?"

"No. If you didn't want to come down here, you wouldn't have told me about the hammer, would you?"

Amos started to say something. Then he realized Dunc was right.

"All right. You win."

"No," Dunc said. "We win. We both win. You'll see, there'll be treasure. I just know it."

Chapter·9

It was just past midnight.

Dunc waited outside Amos's house patiently. There was a special procedure. Amos couldn't come out until his parents went to bed and he heard his father snoring.

Finally Dunc heard scraping and looked down to see Amos crawling out the basement window. His room was in the basement, and he had to use a small ladder and the window didn't open very far so Amos had to squeeze through.

"Now I know how an earthworm feels," he whispered. He scrambled to his feet. "Let's go."

The light from the streetlamp hit his face, and Dunc stopped him. "What happened to your face?"

Both his eyes were swollen, and his nose was all red and puffy. His lower lip was thick looking as well, and he had a cut with square corners on his forehead.

"Oh—Melissa called. I'm sure it was her ring this time. It was about eight o'clock, and we were watching television. I like to get to the phone before the end of that first ring—any sooner, and you look too eager, know what I mean?"

They had their bikes—Amos had fixed his tire—and they pushed them half a block until they were well clear of Amos's house before riding.

"You still didn't tell me what happened," Dunc said.

"So I hear the ring and I make my move," Amos said. "I was sitting on the end of the couch with one leg draped up over the back, you know, all natural."

Dunc nodded.

"Well, I was in good form. I made my roll

backward, missed my mother who was sitting on the end of the couch with both feet, and landed running. I even planned on the cat sleeping near the end of the couch."

They had reached the end of the block, and Dunc swung his leg over the seat on his bike and started riding, fitting his feet into the pedals. "So what happened?"

"Tonka truck." Amos pulled up alongside, the two of them riding slowly. "My little brother left it near the end of the coffee table. I stepped into it on the second step, it rolled, and I didn't make it. The roll carried me to the kitchen doorway, and I almost snagged the phone on the way by, but I grabbed wide and tore it off the wall. I took out my mother's food processor with my face—that's the square cut on my forehead. Luckily it was unplugged. She had it set for puree, and I hit the switch as I dove in. If it had been plugged in, I'd look like baby food about now."

They rode in silence for a time. The way to the waterfront did not go through the downtown section, and Dunc kept them

49

back along the darker sections of the residential areas until they hit the river. Then they followed the river road to the waterfront.

They stopped at the end of the street.

All the streetlights were broken out. It was almost pitch dark except for light leaking out of the tavern about halfway down.

There were only four cars on the whole street, and no signs of any people except noise from the bar.

"Well," Amos said, "I've changed my mind—how about you?"

Dunc ignored him. "I just caught a glimpse of the building with the hammer on it as I left this afternoon."

"You were moving pretty fast."

"So there's this doorway to the right of the building, and it seems to lead into the space between the two buildings. The lock was busted off the hasp."

"You got all this from a glimpse?"

"Well, I was looking for it. I figure if we get in there between the buildings, we should be all right. Then we can find a way into the building and see if there are any clues."

"It's dark," Amos said.

"Yeah, I know. That's why I brought a small flashlight."

Dunc led the way down the right side of the street. They passed an alley, and Amos came up next to him.

"The same guy is there," he said. "With his head under the trash bin. He's not moving."

"He's resting."

"Right."

They made the doorway without incident. Two of the four cars on the street were nearby, but there were no people and no sounds.

Dunc pulled at the door, and it came out slightly, stopped, and he pulled harder.

There was a sound like a cat fight, and the door moved farther on the rusty hinges.

"Stop," Amos said. "Somebody will hear us. . . ."

But Dunc had pulled his bike with him and was already inside. Amos took a quick look up and down the street and followed.

Into a pitch black hole.

"Dunc?" Amos could see nothing.

No answer.

"Dunc?"

Still nothing.

"Dunc!" He whispered it as loudly as he dared.

"Down here—there's a ramp down to a lower level." Dunc whispered from the front and down.

"How about some light?"

"Can't. I dropped the flashlight, and I can't find it. Feel around up there—see if you can locate it."

Amos squatted and swung his fingers back and forth in an arc. He stopped. His hands had hit something, and he jerked back. "Did it have fur on it?"

"Never mind. I found it."

There was a quick flash of light—part of a second—and Amos saw Dunc and his bike down the dirt ramp to the front. They were between two rock walls so old, the cement holding the rocks together was crumbling away.

"Leave your bike. Come on. I found a doorway into the building."

Amos left his bicycle and bounced off the rock wall four times before he found the opening and stepped inside.

Chapter · 10

If anything, it was darker inside the building than it had been outside.

Amos held his hand out and could not see it, moved it closer to his face until his finger was in his eye and still never saw it.

"Dunc?"

"Over here." There was a flash of light—like a flashbulb going off in Amos's eyes—and it was dark again. "Watch out for all the junk."

In the flash, before going stone blind again, Amos had seen Dunc standing in the middle of piles of old tools and cardboard boxes. Then the light had gone off, and there was nothing.

"Come on," Dunc said. "There's a stairway in the back that comes down from upstairs. We're in the basement."

"Dunc, I can't see."

"Go by feel. Move your feet ahead slowly, then take a step."

There was a sudden crashing-clanging.

"What happened?" Dunc whispered.

"I took a step," Amos said. "What do you *think* happened? You know grace isn't my thing. I stepped on a rake, and I think I've got a broken nose."

Dunc sighed. "I'll flash the light, you take a step, then another."

In a series of flashes Amos made his way across the basement through the junk.

"It's like a light show at a concert," he said, finally standing alongside Dunc at the back of the basement. They were under the stairs. "Like a strobe."

"Be quiet—I thought I heard something." Dunc held his hand over Amos's mouth, and the two of them stood but there was no sound.

"All right," Dunc whispered. "Let's go upstairs and see what we can find."

He led the way up the stairs, flicking the light in tiny bursts back down the stairwell so Amos could follow.

At the top there was a door, but it wasn't locked and opened easily.

"Hmmm," Dunc said.

"What?"

"The door—why didn't it squeak?" He leaned down and flashed the light on the hinges. "Look—they've been oiled."

"So?"

"So if this building is abandoned, who's oiling the hinges?"

"So we go home, right?"

"Not yet—let's find out what's upstairs." Dunc moved away from the stairwell door and into the middle of a large room. Along one side there was a counter, and above that were stacks of empty shelves that showed in the flashes of light.

"Looks like an old store," Amos said. He felt his nose and winced. "Man, a rake handle on top of the food processor—noses weren't made for it."

"It might have been a ship chandler's," Dunc said.

"What's that?"

"A store for nautical things. See, there's grease on the shelves—maybe from engine parts. It sure wasn't a tavern."

"Not now—but a long time ago. There might be something somewhere to show what it used to be before it was a chandler's." Amos pointed at the back wall in the darkness. "Shine back there."

Dunc flashed the light on the walls, but they had gone around the room twice before Amos spotted it. And then it was in an image two times before the one they were flashing on.

"Back up one, then another one."

"What?"

"Run the movie backward. I saw some writing."

On the back wall, near the right corner, there were some letters carved in the wood. They showed in the light, and Dunc closed his hand around the flashlight beam so that just a trickle of light came out and they moved into the corner.

" 'D.H. 1857,' " Dunc read. The letters were carved into the old wood of the wall, a cross-board that might have been in back of a bar. "I'll bet it stands for Devil's Hammer. They carved it in the wall back of a bar."

"Yeah," Amos said. "Or it might have been somebody named Donald Hamilton."

"Amos—"

"I know. Be positive, right?"

A sudden clunking sound froze both of them. Dunc turned the light off, and they stood listening, holding their breaths.

There was no repeat of the sound.

"It was a cat," Dunc said.

"Or a rat," Amos said. "As big as a rhino, except that it eats meat. Human flesh. And it's hungry." Amos stopped as he realized he was alone again. "Dunc?"

"Over here." Dunc was moving along the wall, and he held his hand over the light again, letting a tiny stream out. "I'm looking for a tunnel or door. The back of the building is against the stone of the riverbank."

They felt along the wall, tapping, but there was no opening except for the doorway leading to the basement.

"Maybe it's downstairs," Dunc whispered. "And we missed it."

He moved back down the steps and was halfway down when Amos landed on him in a heap that sent both of them tumbling down to the bottom.

"Missed a step," Amos whispered as they untangled themselves. "I was doing all right until that third one. My foot slid over it at a slight angle, and my body weight was past center. I still almost controlled it, but then the main mass of weight caught up and—"

"Amos."

"Right, it doesn't matter. Be quiet. Got it."

"You work one way, I'll work the other." Dunc felt along the wall to the left, and Amos worked to the right. In moments they were back to the stairway.

"Nothing," Dunc said.

"Just rocks and crumbling cement," Amos said. "No tunnels."

"Maybe," Dunc said, "there's a secret passage and a hidden latch that makes a door swing open."

Amos snorted. "Only in movies."

"Then that means there isn't a tunnel." Dunc's voice had a final flatness.

"Yes, well, I told you not to believe a dirty bird."

"So we can go."

"Good. Light my way across the basement so I don't hit that rake again. I'm afraid of that rake."

"How about under the stairs?" Dunc asked suddenly. "What did you find there?"

"That was in your half."

"I thought it was in yours. Come on, let's check it."

Dunc crawled beneath the stairway and halfway back the sliver of light caught it.

There, so low that a person would have to stoop well over to get through it, was a small doorway set into the rock and concrete wall.

Chapter · 11

Amos kneeled next to Dunc. "Is it locked?"

"Just a wooden peg through a hasp." Dunc lifted the peg out and opened the door.

To his surprise, the door swung open easily.

And silently.

He moved the shaft of light to the hinges. "Look—they've been oiled. Just like the hinges upstairs."

"So what?"

"So somebody had to come and do that— they must have had a reason."

"So we go home?"

Dunc snorted. "Not likely. Not now that we've found something."

He pulled the wooden peg and opened the door, crouched down, and crawled in. Amos held for a moment, but the basement was pitch black without the sliver of light from the flashlight, and he kneeled and followed Dunc.

"Close the door," Dunc said, "and I'll turn the flashlight on full."

Amos closed the door, and Dunc took his hand off the light.

The sudden brightness was blinding, and both boys closed their eyes for a second.

"Oh, man, look at this." Dunc opened his eyes and swept the light in front of them. It disappeared down a long tube of darkness.

"It's a tunnel." Amos tried to see the end of it and couldn't. "It must go on forever."

"Just like the parrot said." Dunc flashed the light down and back up, trying to see the end, but the light didn't penetrate far enough.

"I wonder what it was for?"

"Maybe they dug it out for a storeroom or something."

"It's pretty long for a storeroom."

"Who knows? All I know is that it's a tunnel like the bird said, and we've got a shot at buried treasure."

"Maybe it's an old mine," Amos said. "Maybe it goes to the center of the earth."

"It doesn't matter. We go in eight paces and start digging for treasure."

"Tools," Amos said. "We don't have any tools."

"Oh—that's right. How about in the basement? Weren't there some tools there?"

"A rake—that I know about for sure. But I didn't see a shovel."

"Let's go look."

He made a step, and there was a clunking noise from outside and above the tunnel entrance.

"What was that?" Amos said.

"Like before—it was just a rat or cat or something."

There was another thump, then the sound of something being dragged across the floor upstairs, then a thumping as if a heavy weight were being brought down the steps one step at a time.

And then, distinctly, the boys heard a man's voice say:

"I don't care how much we make, I think we should find something lighter than appliances to steal—they barely fit through the door into the tunnel."

"Smuggle," a second man said. "We don't steal—we're smuggling."

Dunc and Amos stood frozen, but Amos broke first.

"Run!" he yelped at Dunc and ran directly over him, headed down the length of the tunnel.

Chapter·12

Dunc had caught up in three jumps and was passing Amos when Amos squeaked:

"The light, kill the light!"

Dunc flipped the switch, and the results were disaster. The two of them were running wide open and went suddenly from bright light to total pitch darkness. Amos went down like an oak, stepping on his own feet, and Dunc fell over him.

"Flick it," Amos whispered. "Flick the light so we can see what we're doing."

Dunc flashed the light, and they were up and running again. He kept flashing it until it showed a side tunnel, smaller than the main run, going off to the right.

"In here!" Dunc swung to the right and Amos bounced off the corner and followed. Just around the corner Dunc stopped. There was another wall with a door, this one slightly larger than the first, but closed. Or it seemed closed at first. There was a crack on the left side, and Dunc tried it.

"Stuck."

"Be quiet," Amos whispered. "They're coming in the tunnel."

Dunc turned off the light again, and the two boys stood silently in the darkness. There was more bumping and cursing, and then a light came down the tunnel, past them, from the doorway.

"Isn't there some better place to store these things while we're waiting to take a load out?" the first man asked.

"I told you—nobody will bother anything here. We need a safe place because it takes so long to get a full load. Now quit griping, and help me."

There was more grunting and cursing. The sound carried well down the tunnel.

"There. Let's get out of here. This place makes my hair stand on end."

"Why? It's just an old powder storage tunnel from the Civil War. They needed a cool, dry place for cannon powder while they were waiting to ship it. Hey, just like us—waiting to ship."

"I still don't like it. It's dark, and there may be spiders."

"All right, all right. Let's go—there's that color television set to pick up yet."

"You think it's safe to go back to the same house?"

"Oh, sure. They're on vacation. We can clean the whole place out. Then we load the truck and take it downstate and sell it at flea markets, just like last time."

"Last time you traded the whole load for old telephone line insulators."

"An investment, my friend. You'll see. Now come on—wait a minute, what's that?"

"What's what?"

"There. Those are tracks heading off down the tunnel. See them in that soft dirt and dust?"

"Tracks?"

"I *told* you I left the peg in the hasp.

Somebody took it out, and they're still in here."

Dunc poked Amos, leaned close to his ear. "Get ready. We have to go through this door. It's our only chance." He pulled Amos up.

The voices came down the tunnel again.

"How do you know they're still here?"

"There's two sets of tracks and they only go one way—they don't come back. And there's no way out of the tunnel. Come on, we've got to find them."

"Oh, come on—they're probably gone. You don't know that there's no other way out. You just walked back a little ways."

"That doesn't matter. I'm not letting anybody steal my stolen appliances."

Dunc leaned close to Amos again and whispered barely loud enough to make a whushing sound. "Ready?"

Amos hesitated. "Well, as a matter of fact—"

"Now!"

Dunc pulled at the door. This time the hinges had not been oiled. The door opened, but with a sound like fingers being dragged down a blackboard. It made a slot wide enough for the two boys, and they wiggled through just as they heard from the tunnel:

"There they are! Come on—let's get 'em!"

Chapter · 13

Dunc stopped just past the door, and Amos ran into him.

"What the—"

"It's a storage room." Dunc flashed the light around. There were barrels and boxes stacked up both sides of the tunnel.

"Let's *go*!" Amos shouted. "They're coming."

"It's powder," Dunc said. "Gunpowder from years ago."

"We have to get going!" Amos dragged him and headed on through the tunnel. "There has to be another way ot here."

"All that powder, all these years." Dunc

followed, and inside forty feet they came to another wooden wall with a narrow door. This door was closed, but Amos got his fingers into the edge and jerked it open, and Dunc and he piled through. Amos closed the door and looked to see Dunc flashing the light.

"It's no good," Dunc said. "It's a dead end."

"No—it can't be."

"It is." Dunc lifted the light. "See? It goes back a little and stops dead."

"What about there—on the side? See it? That low hole?"

Dunc moved the light down and to the right.

There was a small hole—not over three feet in diameter—going off to the side.

They heard a screech as the two men opened the first door on the powder storage room.

"Go for it," Amos said. "We're out of time."

Dunc dived into the small hole, and Amos followed.

Only to be stopped dead in ten feet.

74

"That's it," Dunc said, squirming around. "It ends here—they must have done it to explore a new tunnel and then dropped it."

"We're dead." Amos turned and crouched on all fours. "They've got us."

Dunc said nothing. They held their breath, waiting.

There was a long pause, then they heard:

"My flashlight bulb blew—coming through the door."

"Where are we?"

"I don't know, some sort of room. I've never been in here before, and I didn't see anything before the bulb went."

"Well, keep going—they can't be that far ahead of us."

"I can't. It's pitch dark in here."

"Wait—I'll light a match, and then you go ahead."

"Oh, oh," Amos whispered. "This isn't good, is it?"

The boys heard the scratch of a match, once, twice, then a small whuffing sound as it lit.

"Blow it out!" the other man yelled. "Blow it out! It's pow—"

Which was as far as he got before the powder, stored for 130 years, decided to take over.

There was a huge, deafening barfing sound, a light like fifteen or twenty thousand flashbulbs going off, and Amos and Dunc were driven to the end of the small side tunnel like two corks in a bottle.

"Cover—" Dunc started to yell, was going to yell, *cover your ears* when the shock wave hit them, pounded them, and then there was nothing.

Chapter · 14

Dunc stopped, leaned the shovel against the side of the tunnel, and rubbed his eyes. They were still swollen and a little puffy, and he blinked them a few times to clear them.

Amos also stopped. He'd been digging with a square-shaped garden spade, and now he used it for a prop and took a rest. His eyebrows were starting to grow back, and his hair as well, but it was still short and fuzzy and made him look like a monkey about to ask a question.

The building was gone—blown away from the tunnel mouth by the explosion, and what hadn't been blown away was burned.

"Freak explosions are funny things," Dunc said.

"Oh, yeah," Amos said. "I laughed until I thought I would die."

"No, really. Those two guys hardly got hurt at all because they were right in the center of it."

"They lost all their hair," Amos said. "And all their clothing was blown off, even their shoes and socks. You call that nothing?"

"Well—it could have been worse. The cops told the newspapers that they're starting to hear again, and they can both remember their names now and it's only been two weeks."

The two weeks had been busy. After the fire department had come and the police had found Amos and Dunc out in the street, accompanied by two completely naked men who did not know their names, the newspapers and television had gone crazy.

Dunc's parents had grounded him until he was a grandparent, roughly, and Amos's mother and father had talked about shipping him to the Arctic for a few months, but things had settled.

They had kept the parrot and the story of treasure a secret by saying they had just been exploring the old buildings and had run into the tunnel to hide from the crooks.

And now they had come back.

"They say the washing machine went all the way across the river," Dunc said, picking up his shovel. "It must have come out of that tunnel like a cannonball."

It was the middle of the day, and they had come in on a back street so as to not be noticed.

Amos had wanted to drop it.

"If you think that I'm going to go through all that and *not* get the treasure, you're nuts," Dunc had told Amos. "Whether you come or not, I'm going."

So they were there, and they were digging where the parrot's clues had told them to dig. But it wasn't going well.

"We're down three feet, and there's nothing," Amos said. "I say let's drop it and go play some video games."

Thunk.

Dunc's shovel hit something solid. Dunc looked up, smiling. "See? You were giving up too fast."

Amos grabbed his shovel. "So dig."

The two of them tore into the hole and in a few minutes had uncovered a wooden box. The sides and top were dirty and the outside edges were rotten, but the box was made of oak and seemed sound. It was held closed by a large hasp, but it wasn't locked.

They dragged the box from the hole, set it off to the side. The hasp was rusted in place and Dunc used his shovel to pry it up. Then he used the edge again to pry at the lid, wedged it up, and looked inside.

"What is it?" Amos had been at a wrong angle and came around to see.

"I don't know." Dunc poked in the box with his finger. "It looks like an old rotten sack."

"That's it," Amos said. "Pirates always put their gold in sacks before they buried it. You read about that all over the place."

"Not this time."

"What do you mean?"

"There's nothing in the sack. Well, sort of nothing. There's a rotten gunk, but it's mostly gone. I don't know what—wait, there's something written on the sack."

"What?"

"It's all fuzzy—I can just make it out. It says 'wheat.' Yeah. Wheat."

"The bag had wheat in it?" Amos leaned over, read it. "Wheat—they buried wheat?"

Dunc shook his head. "Crazy, isn't it? Wait—I remember something. During the Civil War this whole area was wiped out. They couldn't get food, and the armies were taking things from the people. I'll bet that was it—the people who were here buried the wheat to keep it safe from the soldiers."

"Wheat?" Amos seemed about to go into shock. "They buried wheat?"

"I guess so."

"So there wasn't a pirate?"

"I guess not."

"And there wasn't a buried treasure?"

"I guess not."

"All of this," Amos said, "all of this with the tunnel and the rats like rhinos and the two crooks and blowing us back into a gopher hole and my eyebrows and hair being gone so I'll *never* be able to talk to Melissa— all of this is for a bag of rotten wheat?"

Dunc nodded. "You know, I just thought of something."

"What?"

"Well—wheat wouldn't be buried treasure to a person. We would think of gold or coins or jewelry—something valuable to us."

"What are you saying?"

"Well—to us it's just wheat. But to somebody else it could be something else. Wheat could be like, well, birdseed. A sack of wheat would be valuable, would be buried treasure—"

"To a parrot," Amos finished. "The parrot was using us. All this time the parrot was just using us to get his birdseed."

Dunc nodded. "It looks that way, doesn't it?"

But he was talking to himself. Amos had dropped his shovel and was walking to his bike.

"Where are you going?"

"To the pet store."

"Amos—wait a minute. Amos, what are you going to do?"

Amos turned and stood, his hands on his handlebars. "I'll give you a hint—it involves a scuzzy parrot and about six pounds of gunpowder." He climbed on his bike and started pedaling.

"Amos, you're kidding, right?" Dunc said. "Now, Amos—don't kill the parrot. Amos. Amos! *Amos!*"

Be sure to join Dunc and Amos in these other Culpepper Adventure/Mystery books:

Dunc's Doll
(Culpepper Adventure/Mystery #2)

Dunc Culpepper and his accident-prone friend Amos are up to their old sleuthing habits once again. This time they're after a band of doll thieves! When a doll that once belonged to Charles Dickens's daughter is stolen from an exhibition at the local mall, the two boys put on their detective gear and do some serious snooping. Will a vicious watch dog keep them from retrieving the valuable missing doll?

Culpepper's Cannon
(Culpepper Adventure/Mystery #3)

Dunc and Amos are researching the Civil War cannon that stands in the town square when they find a note inside telling them about a time portal. Entering it through the dressing room of La Petite, a women's clothing store, the boys find themselves in downtown Chatham on March 8, 1862—the day before the historic clash between the Monitor and the Merrimack. But the Confederate soldiers they meet mistake

them for Yankee spies. Will they make it back
to the future in one piece?

(August 1992)

Dunc Gets Tweaked
(Culpepper Adventure/Mystery #4)

Best friends Dunc and Amos meet up with a
new buddy named Lash when they enter the
radical world of skateboard competition. When
somebody "cops"—steals—Lash's prototype
skateboard, the boys are determined to get it
back. After all, Lash is about to shoot for a to-
tally rad world's record! Along the way they
learn a major lesson: *never* kiss a monkey!

(September 1992)

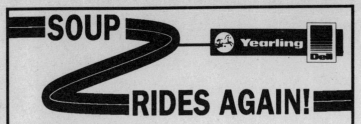

SOUP RIDES AGAIN!

Whether he's riding into trouble on horseback or rolling into trouble on an outrageous set of wheels, Soup and his best friend Rob have a knack for the kind of crazy mix-ups that are guaranteed to make you laugh out loud!

☐ SOUP..48186-4 $3.25

☐ SOUP AND ME 48187-2 $3.25

☐ SOUP FOR PRESIDENT......48188-0 $3.25

☐ SOUP IN THE SADDLE.......40032-5 $3.25

☐ SOUP ON FIRE.....................40193-3 $3.25

☐ SOUP ON ICE 40115-1 $2.75

☐ SOUP ON WHEELS 48190-2 $2.95

☐ SOUP'S DRUM.....................40003-1 $2.95

☐ SOUP'S GOAT 40130-5 $2.95

☐ SOUP'S UNCLE 40308-1 $2.95